I SPY, e-SPY

Janice Greene

SADDLEBACK
PAGETURNERS
• SPY •

PAGETURNERS

SPY

A Deadly Game
An Eye for an Eye
I Spy, e-Spy
Scavenger Hunt
Tuesday Raven

SCIENCE FICTION

Bugged!
Escape From Earth
Flashback
Murray's Nightmare
Under Siege

ADVENTURE

A Horse Called
   Courage
Planet Doom
The Terrible Orchid Sky
Up Rattler Mountain
Who Has Seen
   the Beast?

MYSTERY

The Hunter
Once Upon a Crime
Whatever Happened
   to Megan Marie?
When Sleeping
   Dogs Awaken
Where's Dudley?

Development and Production: Laurel Associates, Inc.
Cover Illustrator: Black Eagle Productions

SADDLEBACK
PUBLISHING · INC.
Three Watson
Irvine, CA 92618-2767
E-Mail: info@sdlback.com
Website: www.sdlback.com

ISBN 1-56254-138-2
Printed in the United States of America
05 04 03 02 01   9 8 7 6 5 4 3 2 1

CONTENTS

Chapter 1

The stranger came into the main computer room a little after midnight. He looked around and spotted Vinnie. As Vinnie walked up to him, the guy shifted his feet restlessly.

"Hi. Do you have a clearance slip?" Vinnie asked politely.

"Don't need no stinkin' clearance slip, man," the guy said carelessly. "I'm just here to update my résumé."

The back of Vinnie's neck burned. The rude tone of the guy's voice said, "You're nothing but a computer operator. I don't need to explain myself to you."

The guy walked over to the row of computer workstations. He looked about 22—not much older than Vinnie. He was tall, with spiky hair and heavy black eyebrows. Vinnie had never seen him before, but that was no surprise. Working the graveyard shift, he hardly got to meet anybody. Most everyone else worked during the day.

Vinnie went back to his newspaper, glancing over at the stranger every few minutes. The guy *said* he was writing his résumé. But why was he thinking of leaving *now*? Websound was due to bring out its hot new program in just three days. It didn't make sense.

Vinnie walked over to the fridge at the back of the big room and got a soda. Catherine, the boss, made sure that the fridge was always well-stocked with sodas and snacks. They were free for everyone, anytime. It was one of the great perks that came with a job at Websound.

Another great thing was the Websound building itself. It was actually an old high school. When Catherine bought it, she had kept the building as it was. So employees had meetings in the auditorium, used the pool for parties, and played basketball up on the roof. Small departments used classrooms. The main computer room, where Vinnie was now, had once been the gym.

Vinnie stared at the stranger's back. As if the guy could feel his eyes, he turned around. Vinnie quickly looked away, sipping his soda as if he didn't have a thought in his head.

"If anyone brings out a first-class music program before we do, we're dead. It's that simple." That's what Catherine had told Vinnie when he was hired. "This is Websound's first big product, and if it doesn't succeed, we don't have the money to launch a second."

Websound's program was called SoundUp. With it, you could download music from the Internet. Vinnie knew several companies were racing to produce a program like SoundUp. A fortune could be made by selling such a program to record companies. Whoever reached the finish line first had it made. SoundUp, he'd been told, had a good chance of being the winner. Its launch date had been set for the day after tomorrow.

Vinnie walked soundlessly back toward his chair, studying the stranger. He was hunched over the keyboard, his mouth open. Even at a distance, Vinnie could see the slight rise and fall of his shoulders. He was breathing hard.

Vinnie's thoughts whirled. What was going on? The guy looked excited or scared—or both. Something wasn't right. He bent over the paper, pretending to be completely absorbed in the sports page.

After a few minutes, he heard a faint but unmistakable sound. *The guy was putting a disk in the diskette drive of the computer.*

"Anyone bringing in a disk from outside is fired—period," Catherine had told him. "We can't afford to risk either a virus or theft."

Vinnie got up noisily, rattling the

paper and heading toward the restroom. He went inside and closed the stall door with a slam. Then he waited a moment and sneaked out without making a sound. He walked quietly down the hall to one of the former classrooms.

Closing the door, he picked up the phone and dialed security.

"Terrell," he said quietly, "there's a guy in here who's downloading stuff to a disk. When he leaves, I'll follow a little behind, and you catch him at the door."

"Right," said Terrell. "And Vinnie— you keep your distance, just in case. Leave the heavy stuff to me."

Vinnie hung up. He thought he heard a soft noise outside the door. Opening it quickly, he was about to look around outside. But just then the stranger charged at him—his arm raised over his head! Vinnie swerved. But something scraped his ear and struck him heavily on the shoulder. He grunted with pain and went down.

# Chapter 2

Vinnie lay on the floor, his shoulder throbbing. The stranger's feet were in front of his face. Then, in one swift move, Vinnie reached out and grabbed the stranger behind the knees, pulling the guy over on top of him.

Before his attacker could right himself, Vinnie rolled over hard— slamming the guy to the floor. His head went down with a solid thump.

"Freeze, man! Hold it right there!" Terrell was standing in the doorway. "Don't you even blink!" The security guard ran up and bent over the stranger. He pressed the cold metal of his pistol against the man's cheek.

"*Terrell!*" cried Vinnie. "I didn't even hear you come up here."

Terrell grinned. "I've got cat feet," he said. "Nobody hears me when I don't want to be heard."

Vinnie saw a bronze paperweight shaped like a dolphin lying on the floor. When he touched his wounded ear, his fingers came away bloody.

Terrell waved his gun at the stranger. "Get up!" he ordered.

The man slowly staggered to his feet, rubbing the back of his head.

Terrell's strong, skinny arms reached out for the stranger's chest, as if he was about to frisk him.

The man held up his hands. "No way! You don't even have the right to touch me!" he panted. "I want a lawyer. I'm not saying anything until I have a lawyer."

"Stay with him, Terrell," said Vinnie. "I'm going to check out his desk."

Vinnie jogged back to the desk where the stranger had been working. The screen said, *SoundUp Master File download successful.* There was no disk in sight, but the message on the screen was enough. The stranger had been downloading the new SoundUp program!

Vinnie went back to Terrell and the stranger. "Keep an eye on him," he told the guard. "I'm calling Catherine."

When Vinnie returned, Terrell was sitting in a chair, his gun pointed at the prisoner. The stranger sat on the floor in front of him. Without actually moving, he was trying to lean away from the gun as far as possible.

"Catherine will be here as soon as she can," Vinnie told Terrell.

They waited, Terrell and his prisoner never taking their eyes from each other.

Finally, Terrell said, "Vinnie, tell me something. There's all kinds of programs to get music off the Internet. What's so different about SoundUp? Why have we got slimeballs like this guy here breaking in on us? Or can you give me the lowdown in front of this loser?"

"Okay, Terrell. You know how

everyone used to download music for free—and then bands started suing? Well, with SoundUp, the performers get paid what they're owed."

"Royalties," said the stranger.

"Shut up, *scum!*" Terrell growled. "We don't need any lecture from you."

Then Vinnie went on. "When you use SoundUp to download a song, exactly the right amount of money is sent to the record company and the performers. Websound has it worked out for every country where the music is sold. Do you see how amazing that is? That's why SoundUp is so valuable."

The prisoner shifted uneasily on the floor. "Keep still, loser," said Terrell, "and wait for your punishment."

Not more than 20 minutes later, Catherine arrived. She was about 40, small and trim, with bright blond hair. She looked tired—but she was dressed, as always, as if she were going to a classy restaurant. She was the only one at

Websound who didn't wear jeans. Her eyes widened when she saw Vinnie's ear.

"Are you okay?" she asked.

"I'm not really hurt," said Vinnie. "It's just messy looking."

"Not just your ear. How about the rest of you?" said Catherine.

"Just a few bruises—that's it," Vinnie said.

"Okay, tell me what happened," said Catherine. "You, too, Terrell."

When they finished, Catherine sat down in front of the stranger. Her dark blue eyes looked as deep as the ocean, and just about as cold.

"Give me the disk. Then—if you tell me where you're from and who sent you— I won't call the police," said Catherine.

The stranger raised a thick eyebrow. "You won't call anyway," he said with a sneer. "You call the cops and you're admitting that someone got past your security. Do you get my drift, lady? You're admitting failure."

Catherine thought about that. "Maybe not at this point," she said. "Could be a little publicity right now makes it very clear to the record companies that our program is the best one—the only one that's really worth stealing."

A bead of sweat trickled down the stranger's cheek.

Catherine went on. "Let's see—you're up for assault," she said, lifting her head to stare at him. "For theft, for breaking and entering . . . "

"Not breaking and entering!" said the stranger. "I had an ID card."

"Where'd you get it?" Catherine asked.

The stranger swallowed. There was a long silence.

"Assault with a weapon is a *felony*," Catherine went on. "I'd say you're looking at 15 years, at least."

The stranger looked sick, but he said nothing.

"Then there's theft of property worth

several million dollars. And don't forget that's theft with a weapon involved. "

The stranger glared at Catherine. With an angry growl, he took a disk out of his pocket and shoved it at her.

"*And* your ID card," said Catherine.

The stranger handed it over.

"Thank you," Catherine said. She put the ID card and the disk in her purse. "Okay, who sent you?"

The stranger was silent.

Catherine took her cell phone from her purse. She raised an eyebrow at the stranger, as if giving him a last chance.

"All right! I'm from Keyboard!" he cried angrily. "Some management guy said they'd pay me real well if I did it. He gave me the ID card. I never even met the guy before—which is the way they wanted it."

"I suppose they offered you so much money you couldn't possibly refuse," said Catherine with dry sarcasm.

She turned to Terrell. "That's all I

needed to know. Get rid of this guy."

"Come on, slimeball," said Terrell. He roughly pulled the guy to his feet.

"*Gently*, Terrell," Catherine insisted. "Take the man to the front door, say goodnight, and let him go."

Terrell and the stranger left.

Catherine leaned forward, rubbing her temples. She looked exhausted.

"Tell me something, Catherine. Is it really a felony to whack someone with a paperweight?" said Vinnie.

"I don't know," Catherine said, with a faint smile.

"Someone here at Websound was probably in on this deal, right?" Vinnie asked. "Otherwise it would be pretty hard to get an ID."

"It would seem so," Catherine said.

"Why don't we check out the ID and see if it shows up any clues? It probably won't—if the guy was smart enough—but it's worth a try," said Vinnie. "Then we could search for the password he used to get into the computer files."

Catherine looked at Vinnie with new interest.

"Are you interested in computer security?" she asked.

"I sure am!" said Vinnie. "I'm taking criminal justice classes at City College. This is my second year."

Catherine was silent for a minute. Then she smiled. "You're a hero, Vinnie. My first thought was to have you come to the office tomorrow and give you a standing ovation. But I've got a better idea. How'd you like to work for Ken Castle, our security manager?"

Vinnie gasped. He wanted to hug her. *"Fantastic!"* he managed to say.

"Why don't you come to my office tomorrow at noon?" said Catherine. "We won't mention the visit from our snoop tonight. We won't even let people know you're reporting to Ken. We'll put you with the development team and say you're doing a special project for me.

That way you can keep an eye on everyone. How does that sound?"

"You won't be sorry, Ms. Cochran!" Vinnie exclaimed.

They shook hands. Vinnie couldn't stop grinning.

He was still floating on air when he checked in at the receptionist's desk the next day. He'd hardly slept at all. Vinnie's dad was a roofer somewhere in Texas. His mom and sister were clerks in a drugstore. His family could sure use some extra help with money.

"Vincent Torres?" the receptionist inquired. "Have a seat. Catherine got called into a meeting, so Joelle's going to show you around."

"Joelle?" said Vinnie.

The door opened. "I'm Joelle," said a young woman about Vinnie's age. "I'm the intern for Development."

Vinnie got up and shook her hand, trying not to stare too hard. Joelle was really cute. She had light brown eyes and hair that fell in long, soft waves.

"I'll show you your desk," she said. She led him into the gym, where he worked every night. Now it was full of people. Most of the guys had their feet on their desks, their keyboards in their laps. Two women were throwing a Nerf football in the back of the room. A large box of donuts, half empty, sat open on a table next to a coffeepot.

"You're going to love it here!" Joelle said. "We work hard—but we play a lot, too." She introduced him to the group. A guy named Cisco signed him up for noontime basketball on the roof.

"I'm in!" Vinnie thought to himself.

Joelle took him to the same desk where the stranger had been sitting. It was empty now. She gave him a headset for his phone and helped him set up his voicemail.

Vinnie sneaked glances at her as she bent over the phone. She was definitely a looker, he thought. But he was keeping his distance until he found out whether she had a good personality. His last girlfriend had been a looker, too. But in the end she'd treated him like a pesky insect that needed to be squashed.

"I'm supposed to take you in to see Ken Castle now," said Joelle. "He's probably going to lecture you about the importance of tight security. SoundUp's about to launch, you know."

She took him down the hall, past the auditorium. At last they reached a row of offices. Catherine's office was here, and the offices of some other people Vinnie didn't know. All the offices except Ken Castle's had glass doors. His was built of solid wood.

"See you later," said Joelle.

Two minutes later, Vinnie had forgotten all about her. He was too excited. Being teamed up with a guy like Ken Castle was his *dream*—because a man like Ken Castle was everything he wanted to be.

# Chapter 3

"Come on in," a deep voice called out in response to Vinnie's knock.

Vinnie opened the door and stepped inside. The office was spare and modern. The walls were decorated with posters of old-fashioned movies. Ken Castle got up and moved around his wide desk to shake Vinnie's hand.

He was well-dressed and darkly tan. Vinnie figured that the man's haircut must have cost more than Vinnie's one good pair of shoes.

"So you're the man of the hour!" Ken said with a broad smile. "You know you saved me a couple of million last night?"

"I was pretty lucky, I guess," said Vinnie modestly.

"Don't sell yourself short," said Ken.

"You pulled off a good one—a big-time move. Now you get what's owed you. Take it—and no apologies!" said Ken.

"Uh—it's good to move up from my old job," said Vinnie.

Ken nodded. "That was a nothing job," he said. "You're too smart for that."

Vinnie grinned.

Ken said, "Forget what your mom told you about sharing and caring and being a nice guy. Right now, Web commerce is the gold rush. I'm telling you, Vinnie, it's pioneer days! But there's only so much gold. The game is to get in fast, and get what you can. And if some guy steals from your claim— shoot him!" Ken aimed his finger like a gun and mimicked pulling a trigger.

Vinnie gulped. "I guess you're right," he said.

The older man leaned back in his chair. "Okay, tell me your ideas. How are we going to nail this claim jumper?"

"I'd check out his ID card, which

23

probably won't tell us anything," Vinnie said. "And I'd *especially* check out where the guy was working."

"That computer hasn't been touched since our would-be thief got in," Ken said. "I haven't even looked at it."

Vinnie went on. "I'd see if we can find out what password the guy was using. Then we should check everyone's files. Maybe we can find a connection between the thief and someone who's working here."

"You are *good!*" Ken cried. "We're going to trap this mole, aren't we, Vinnie? Then we'll get SoundUp out there ahead of the competition and make an outrageous amount of money, right?"

"Right!" said Vinnie.

Ken held out his palm and Vinnie slapped it. He couldn't believe it. This was the best day of his life.

After the interview, Vinnie had the rest of the day off. He decided to treat himself to lunch at Tia's, a popular lunch place half a block from the office.

Joelle was there, eating a salad. She smiled when she saw him. Vinnie relaxed. It wasn't a weird smile, like she couldn't wait to mess with his head. It wasn't a predatory smile, like she was the shark and he was lunch. It was a warm, welcoming smile.

"Don't tell me you're one of those women who eat nothing but salad and yogurt," Vinnie teased.

"Nah," she laughed. "My burger's on the way. Are you one of those guys who *never* eats anything green?"

"Oh, no. I always insist on a piece of lettuce with my burger," said Vinnie.

"Oh, you're one of those real health nuts," said Joelle with a grin.

Before this, it hadn't even occurred to Vinnie to think about Joelle in a romantic way. But for some reason the words just popped out of his mouth: "Do you have—uh—some guy you're seeing?" he asked.

"Yeah . . . " said Joelle.

Vinnie heard hesitation in her voice. "But I take it that it's not the romance of the century?" he said.

"We're having some problems," she said. "We're trying to work things out."

"Uh-huh," said Vinnie. "Is *he* trying to work things out, too?"

"Of course!" said Joelle. "So tell me. How was your meeting with Ken?"

"Great!" said Vinnie. "He seems to be a really amazing guy!"

Joelle frowned. "He's pretty full of himself."

"Yeah, but who wouldn't be when you're such a success?" said Vinnie.

"He's *supposed* to be smart," Joelle said grudgingly, "but he's really into money—money and power."

"Isn't that what everyone wants?" said Vinnie.

"I don't!" Joelle cried. "When I was in high school, I used to have dumb little jobs like selling shoes. But now I've got a job that really *means* something. It's creative, it challenges me, and the people are wonderful. I'd almost work at Websound for free! I can't imagine Ken ever saying something like that."

"Maybe not. But I bet Ken's really creative," said Vinnie.

Joelle frowned. "You know that saying you see on bumper stickers—*The one who dies with the most toys wins?* That's Ken's philosophy."

"What's wrong with that?" Vinnie laughed. "Everybody wants nice things, even if they don't admit it."

"What about balance? If all you want are *things*, you're dead already!" said Joelle, her voice rising.

"That's easy for you to say. Maybe you've never been poor!" said Vinnie.

"Poor in what? *Values?*" said Joelle.

They glared at each other. Vinnie had a sinking feeling somewhere between his throat and his stomach. What was happening? He hadn't wanted their conversation to go like this at all.

"I better get back to work," Joelle mumbled. Then she got up and hurried out the door, just as the waiter brought her burger! Vinnie decided he wasn't hungry either. What a bummer. There was nothing to do but go home to the dark little apartment he shared with his sister and her two noisy kids.

The next day, Vinnie started looking through everyone's files and watching the people around him. Who was the mole, he wondered? There was skinny Cisco, who always wore his headset so he could listen to Vinnie's favorite band, "Street Soldiers." There was goofy Kyle, who had more than a dozen little plastic monsters on his desk. There was Danny, a young guy everyone called "Dude," who was always asking questions. There were Kirsten and Elizabeth, who tossed around a Nerf football at every break. They all seemed to be harmless computer nerds. Vinnie couldn't imagine any of them plotting to steal SoundUp.

After lunch, Vinnie saw Joelle headed his way. He quickly switched to another screen so she couldn't see that he was searching her e-mail.

"Hi," she said.

"Hi, Joelle," Vinnie answered.

Joelle looked down at the floor. Then she said, "Uh—about yesterday. Don't get me wrong. I don't want you to think I live in an empty room and give away all my birthday presents."

Vinnie smiled. "And I don't want *you* to think I'm planning to be buried in my Mercedes."

Joelle laughed. "I've seen you talking to everybody. You're a nice guy."

"You're right about the people here," said Vinnie. "They're great."

Kyle called across the room, "Hey, Joelle, can you help me with this dumb fax machine? It's making a funny clicking noise again."

"You computer geniuses," Joelle

laughed. "I bet you can't run a toaster." She gave Vinnie a quick smile and walked off toward Kyle's desk.

Vinnie turned back to checking out Joelle's e-mail. He saw that she had sent a message to someone named Brad at a company called Keyboard. Vinnie frowned. Keyboard was where the stranger worked.

Vinnie opened the e-mail and read: "20k is acceptable, but SoundUp disk must be in our offices by 11 P.M. Friday night — B."

Vinnie read the message over and over, until his eyes blurred. He couldn't believe it. Joelle was the mole!

Chapter 4

"What? *Joelle's* the mole?" Ken cried. He shook his head in disbelief. "Why, that's hard to imagine, isn't it?"

"Yeah!" said Vinnie. "I can't believe she'd do something like that! She seems so nice . . . I mean, I haven't known her that long, but—"

"You like her," Ken said with a knowing smile.

"I guess it's obvious," said Vinnie.

"Oh, not really," said Ken. "I'm fairly skilled at reading people, that's all."

"I feel sick," said Vinnie.

Ken leaned over his desk, his light blue eyes boring into Vinnie's. "Look, Vinnie, this is no time to go soft. Facts are facts. This girl is a traitor, and she's got to hang for it."

"A *traitor*," Vinnie said softly.

"What a guy! You're a hero—again!" Ken whooped. "What are you gonna ask Catherine for?"

Vinnie just stared at him.

"Get a raise! A bonus!" Ken cried. "Remember what I said? You gotta *take* what's coming to you." He made a grasping motion in the empty air. "Now, tell Catherine you need to see her."

When Vinnie told Catherine that Joelle was the mole, she winced as if the words hurt her. "Joelle!" she cried. "But that can't be true! Give me a few minutes, Vinnie. I'd like to talk to Joelle privately." As he walked out the door, he saw Catherine bending over her keyboard and shaking her head as she messaged Joelle to come to her office.

Vinnie went back to his desk and sat, staring at the computer screen. He kept imagining Joelle covering her face, her shoulders shaking with sobs.

In just a few minutes, a message

appeared on Vinnie's screen. Catherine wanted him in her office ASAP.

Catherine sat behind her desk, her face tight. Joelle sat in a chair against the wall, looking shaken and angry. She glared at Vinnie as he came in.

"Joelle denies having anything to do with Keyboard," Catherine said. "Show us this e-mail you saw, please." She got up from her desk, and Vinnie sat down in front of her computer.

Vinnie worked his way into Joelle's e-mail. He hated doing this in front of her—but what choice did he have? His mind clouded with confusion. Joelle had seemed so *honest* when she talked about Websound! She'd made him believe that she *loved* working there. How could anyone put on an act like that?

He couldn't find the e-mail. So he started over again, feeling both women's eyes boring into his back.

Again, he searched the screen. But the message simply wasn't there. It was gone. His hands started to shake.

"Well?" Catherine's voice was cold.

"Let me try something else," said Vinnie, his voice thick with tension. He told himself to slow down.

But it had disappeared. The e-mail he'd read just minutes ago was gone.

He turned to Catherine. "It's not there," he said slowly.

Catherine closed her eyes for a moment. There was a long silence until she finally said, "Vinnie, I'm disappointed. I don't know what your game is—but it seems that ambition may have gotten the best of you. I can't have a valuable worker like Joelle falsely accused. Please clean out your locker immediately. We'll mail your final check to your home."

Vinnie was stunned. He turned to the door, dropping his gaze as Joelle's angry eyes met his. He walked around to the back of the gym so no one would see him. Numb with shock, he got his jacket from his locker.

He took the bus home and stared at the TV until his eyes hurt. Later, when Olivia and the kids came home, he retreated to his room. After a while, Olivia knocked on the door.

"Are you okay in there?" she asked.

"Sure, sis. I've just got a headache," said Vinnie.

"Want some dinner?" Olivia asked.

"No thanks, Livie. I'll get myself something later," he said.

The kids, Marisol and Robbie, started yelling in the background. "You two just shut up—and I mean *now!*" hollered Olivia. "Uncle Vinnie's got a headache and he needs quiet!" She stomped off down the hall.

Vinnie got up and found the phone book. Ken Castle wasn't listed. He called directory assistance.

"Hello, do you have a Kenneth Castle on Slayton Street?" said Vinnie.

"No," said the operator. "Let's see. I have only one Kenneth Castle listed—but he's listed on Larchmont Drive."

"Oh, that's it—Larchmont!" said Vinnie. "Number 12 Larchmont, right?"

"No, sir. The listing I have is for 111 Larchmont," said the operator.

"That must be it then. I'll try that," Vinnie said. "Thank you."

He dialed Ken Castle's number, and the man answered on the first ring.

"Hello," Ken said pleasantly.

Vinnie hung up. He didn't want to talk on the phone. He didn't even know what he wanted to say. Yet he wanted to see Ken—to be close to his strength and energy. Ken was smart. If anyone could help him out of the hole he was in, Ken was the one.

Vinnie got his jacket and asked Olivia to borrow her car.

Twenty minutes later he was lost. He pulled over and looked at the map. He'd never been in the hilly part of town before. The houses up here were large, separated by broad green lawns.

Vinnie drove on and finally saw a sign for Larchmont Drive. It was a wide, winding road that led up a steep hill. As he drove farther up, the houses got bigger and cars on the street became fewer and fewer. Lights in the windows showed that these houses were two—even three—stories tall. And all of them were new. A few lawns and trees had been planted, but some yards were still bare dirt. Vinnie drove slowly along the silent street. Peeking between the houses, he could see the lights of the gritty, crowded downtown area twinkling far below.

There it was, 111 Larchmont Drive. It was a three-story house on a bare lot. The garage was wide enough for three cars. In the driveway was a sailboat. Vinnie bet it was as new as the house. Maybe, he thought, just maybe, it was as new as the SoundUp program. A wave of anger and hurt went through him. He slammed his fist against the dashboard until his hand throbbed.

Chapter 5

Vinnie sat in front of Ken's house for a long time. Then a patrol car drove slowly down the block. Vinnie realized he'd better get Olivia's scruffy little Ford moving before the cop got suspicious.

When he passed the cop, the patrol car slowed, but let him go by.

The next day at noon, he was waiting at Tia's. Finally, after an hour, Joelle came in. She took one look at him and turned around. Vinnie jumped up from his chair and hurried after her.

"Joelle!" said Vinnie.

"Stay away from me. I don't want to talk to you," Joelle snapped.

"Joelle, *please*," said Vinnie. "Give me five minutes. I just want to apologize. Then I'll leave, and you don't ever have to see my stupid face again."

Joelle's tense look softened. She nodded her head and said, "Okay."

They sat down. Vinnie took a deep breath and the words poured out of him. "When I saw that e-mail to Keyboard yesterday, I felt horrible because you're really nice, and I really like you. I was shocked, too—because from what you told me, selling out is against everything you believe in. But I *had* to accuse you, because I honestly thought you'd done it. The evidence was there! Now I know it wasn't you, and I'm really sorry."

Joelle stared at the table, showing no expression. Vinnie got up to leave.

"Vinnie, wait a minute," she finally said. "If you're sure you saw that e-mail, how do you think it got there?"

"I think Ken did it so I could see it," said Vinnie. "Then after—"

"*Ken?*" Joelle gasped.

"He's got a huge house way up in the hills. Looks like it's brand new. And

39

a fancy new boat, too," said Vinnie.

"Maybe he inherited it," said Joelle.

"Has he recently mentioned someone dying in his family?" Vinnie asked. "Do you remember him taking time off to go to a funeral?"

"No, I don't think so," said Joelle.

"Have you ever been to Catherine's house?" Vinnie asked.

"Just a couple of times. You know, for staff parties," Joelle replied.

"Is it a three-story castle with a boat parked outside?" Vinnie asked.

"No, nothing like that," said Joelle.

"Of all the people at Websound, who do you think is actually capable of selling out?" said Vinnie.

"Look," she said, "Ken loves money— but that doesn't make him a crook."

"Well, I'm certain that he *planted* that e-mail for me to see. Then he deleted it before I went to see Catherine. Who else could have done that?"

"You're just speculating, Vinnie.

None of that is actual proof," Joelle said. But Vinnie could see that she was halfway convinced. "I'd better get back now," she said, looking at her watch.

"But you haven't eaten anything," Vinnie pointed out. "Come on. At least let me buy you a sandwich."

Joelle shook her head. "Vinnie," she said, "you just lost your job. You shouldn't be buying me anything."

"I want to anyway," said Vinnie. "Come on and choose something."

"You're crazy," she laughed, but her voice was warm and friendly.

She called the waitress over and ordered a chicken sandwich to go.

"Give me five more minutes and eat it here—*please*?" Vinnie begged.

"Vinnie!" she said, shaking her head. Then she smiled. "Okay," she said. "Then I've really got to go."

"You're right," Vinnie said. "We need some kind of proof to use against Ken. We've got to get to his files."

Joelle gulped on a bite of sandwich. "What do you mean, '*we*'?"

"Come on! I can't do it without you, Joelle," Vinnie pleaded.

"There is absolutely no way to get into Ken's files. He's set up some incredible kind of security system."

"Ever hear of Kevin Mitnick, the legendary hacker?" said Vinnie.

"Sure," said Joelle.

"Mitnick said the weakest link in the security chain is the human element. He didn't break into systems by bypassing security. He *talked* people into giving him their passwords," said Vinnie.

"Ha! Ken will *never* give you his password," said Joelle. "He's not stupid."

Vinnie said, "Then we need to find his weak spot."

"He doesn't *have* a weak spot," Joelle insisted. "He's an insensitive guy. He doesn't care about anybody—"

"That's *it!*" said Vinnie. "His ego."

Joelle got up. "Now I *really* have to

get going," she said, shaking her head.

Vinnie put his hand on her arm. "Meet me here after work, okay?" said Vinnie. "Until then, I'll be thinking hard."

"Okay," Joelle said with a sigh. "But don't forget that Kevin Mitnick spent almost five years in prison!"

Chapter 6

By the time Joelle met Vinnie after work, he had a plan all worked out.

"An *interview*!" Joelle cried. "I can't do that!"

"Sure you can," said Vinnie. "It'll be easy—because he'll love it."

"How can you be so sure that would work?" said Joelle.

"I'm not," Vinnie admitted cheerfully. "But the more we know about him, the better chance we have of figuring out a password."

"I could use my sister's cell phone," she said slowly. "Nobody can recognize my voice on it."

"Then you'll do it?" said Vinnie.

Joelle nodded, her lips pursed. "Catherine got a press release from

Keyboard this afternoon. Their software's coming out the day after tomorrow, too. And this is terrible, Vinnie—their description makes it sound exactly like SoundUp! Everybody's just sick about it. Catherine's really upset. Every night she's been taking the master disk and locking it in this little safe in her office."

"Good. That should make it harder for him," said Vinnie.

They agreed to meet back at the restaurant two hours later. Joelle arrived late, looking nervous. Vinnie had written out a whole script for her on a napkin.

She yanked the cell phone out of her purse and slid it across the table. Vinnie reached out to take her hand.

Joelle pulled her hand away. "Don't, Vinnie," she said nervously.

"Slow down," he said. "You're gonna trap Ken Castle, and you're gonna save Websound. Now take a deep breath and I'll dial the number for you."

Vinnie punched in the numbers and

handed her the cell phone.

"Hello?" Ken answered on the first ring. "Ken Castle speaking."

Joelle closed her eyes and said, "Mr. Castle? Good evening. This is Sasha Colvin from *The Courier*. I'm hoping you can help me with a story I'm writing about your new music software. I'm calling you because I've been told that you can actually put a sentence together—unlike some of these computer types—"

Ken laughed. "I know what you mean. It's sad. You get some of these nerds away from their computers and they can't even fend for themselves."

"Anyway," Joelle went on, "I've been asking around. Everyone says that you're the one who really knows what's going on at Websound."

"Well, in all modesty—they're right," said Ken. "I—" He broke off.

Joelle heard a dog whining in the background.

"Yes?" she said.

"Ah, where was I?" said Ken.

"You were telling me that you knew what was going on," said Joelle. Again, she heard the dog whine.

"Look, I've got to go now," said Ken. "Why don't you call Lester Fong at LiquidSound? He's pretty good."

Joelle looked across the table at Vinnie and made a what-do-I-do-now face. Vinnie squirmed in his chair, wondering what was going on.

"Is something wrong with your dog?" said Joelle. She made her voice sound warm and concerned.

"She just had surgery on her hip," said Ken. "I think she's uncomfortable."

"Come here, baby," he called to the dog. "Tell Daddy what's wrong."

"Oh, your poor poochie!" said Joelle. "What's her name?"

"It's Mignon," said Ken. "The word means 'cute' in French."

Joelle's eyes widened excitedly. "Oh,

that's a wonderful name," she said. "I'll let you go now so you can take care of her. And I'll call Mr. Fong right away. Thanks so much for your help!"

She hung up. "*Mignon!*" she cried. "That's gotta be his password. He sounds really crazy about his dog."

Vinnie stood up. "Sounds like a good place to start. I'm going to try to get to the bottom of this tonight," he said.

"Wait a minute. I want to come with you," said Joelle.

"You sure?" Vinnie asked.

Joelle nodded. Vinnie bent down and gave her a quick kiss on the cheek.

"Hey!" she said. "Watch it, Torres."

Vinnie grinned. "Any way we can get into the building without breaking in?" he asked.

"Not a ghost of a chance," said Joelle. "Catherine just made the announcement today: Nobody's allowed in the building after regular working hours until SoundUp is released."

"Okay," said Vinnie. "Do you know if they fixed that cracked window yet?"

"I don't know. Let's find out," said Joelle. She glanced out the window. "Look—the 41 bus is coming. Let's go!"

About 15 minutes later, they were on the sidewalk outside the Websound building. One of the classroom windows had been cracked a couple of weeks ago. Someone had thrown a shoe at it. Cisco and Elizabeth had found the shoe lying in the bushes. But Catherine had been too busy with the release of SoundUp to get the window repaired.

Tall bushes grew under the windows. Vinnie waded into the tangled branches beneath the window and started to climb. Branches and twigs snapped under his weight. "Push me up," he panted. "This thing won't hold me."

Joelle pushed her way toward Vinnie, twigs slapping her face. She shoved at the backs of his legs.

Grunting, Vinnie finally reached the

windowsill and hauled himself up onto the skinny ledge.

"Car coming!" Joelle hissed. "Stay put. I'll do something to distract them."

She ran out to the sidewalk. Just as the headlights hit the building, she stood nonchalantly, glancing at her watch. Vinnie watched, his breath tight and his heart pumping hard.

The car pulled up to Joelle, and a window rolled down.

"Hey, pretty lady," said a man's deep voice. "Sup?"

"Nothing much," said Joelle. "My husband and I are out walking the dog." She sounded completely calm.

"I don't see no husband or no dog," the guy said with a little laugh.

"He took the dog around the side of the building to do his thing," she said.

The guy chuckled and nodded. "Okay, baby. Later," he said as he gunned his engine and drove on.

Joelle ran back to the side of the

building. Vinnie was pulling a long triangle of glass from the window.

"Joelle!" he said with a little laugh, "for an honest person, you're about the best liar I've ever seen."

"Thank you—I think," Joelle said. "Hand me the glass. . . . Ouch!"

"Careful!" said Vinnie. "What'd you do? Let's see."

"It's just a little cut," said Joelle. "I must have grabbed it wrong."

"Your boyfriend's not gonna like you getting cut up in the line of duty," Vinnie said.

"Shut up and duck!" said Joelle. "Here comes another car."

Vinnie crouched down low, and Joelle dropped behind the bush as the car moved on down the street.

"Oh, brother! This is gonna take all night," Joelle complained.

"No, it's just gonna *seem* like it's taking all night," said Vinnie. "Ouch!" he added, wiping a cut on his sweatshirt.

They both had several small scrapes and cuts on their arms by the time the window was finally emptied of glass. Vinnie laid his sweatshirt on the window sill to protect them from any remaining slivers of glass.

Then he held onto Joelle's shoulders and looked seriously into her face. "Do you understand what this means, Joelle? Everything we do from now on— well, we're breaking the law. . . ."

"I know that," said Joelle. "Let's go."

Chapter 7

Joelle led the way, and Vinnie stayed close behind her. They crawled in the window and dropped to the floor with a loud thump.

"*Oof!*" said Vinnie, as quietly as he could. "Let's wait a minute. Terrell might have heard that."

"Does he walk around a lot?" Joelle asked in a low voice.

"Not much," said Vinnie. "Usually, he just stays in his office, watching the security camera screens."

"What do we do about the cameras in the gym?" said Joelle.

"We'll hope Terrell is getting a cup of coffee," Vinnie whispered.

They walked down the dark hallway toward the gym. Every sound they made seemed very loud—even their breathing.

Vinnie opened the heavy door to the gym, and they hurried inside. The big room was nearly dark, but the lights from the outdoor pool shone brightly in the windows. The blue plastic sheet over the pool made an eerie green glow in the glare of the yellow lights.

Vinnie headed for Kirsten's desk. It was a mess—piled high with papers, books, empty chip bags, and two Nerf footballs. It would be hard for anyone to spot them behind the clutter.

"You start looking," said Vinnie. "I'll keep an eye out for Terrell."

Joelle sat down and started up the computer. When the password prompt came up, she typed in "mignon."

Ken's files opened up immediately. *"Yesss!"* she whispered excitedly.

She went to the e-mail folder right away. It was huge.

"Okay, now do a quick search," said Vinnie nervously. "You need to look for anything from Keyboard. . . . "

"I know!" hissed Joelle.

The search showed nothing. "I'm going to have to open up every e-mail message," she said. Her fingers flew as she checked one message after another.

Suddenly the circular beam of a flashlight covered them. "Gotcha! Stand up real slow now. Both of you!" Terrell's voice boomed out behind them. Vinnie's breath caught in his throat. He had never heard Terrell make a sound.

"Vinnie Torres!" Terrell cried. "I don't believe it!" He looked disgusted. His flashlight and his gun were pointed at Vinnie's chest.

"Come on, Terrell," Vinnie said. "It's not what you think!"

"Don't start!" said Terrell. "I'm not hearing any sorry excuses. You got no good reason to be here. *None!*"

"Listen, Terrell. Ken Castle's trying to rob us! Just wait a minute and we'll show you," said Joelle.

"Ken Castle?" Terrell cried. "Don't give me that. No way he's a crook."

Anger flared in Vinnie's chest. "I'm really surprised at you, Terrell. How come it's so darn easy for you to believe that *I'm* a crook and that Ken Castle isn't? Maybe it's because he's a rich Anglo guy and I'm not?"

"No!" Terrell cried. "It's because he's not breaking into my building!"

He put the flashlight on the desk. "Now just shut up, both of you! Stand over there against the wall."

Vinnie and Joelle moved to the wall. Terrell pulled his cell phone out of his pocket and started punching in numbers. Vinnie noticed that his shoulder was about a foot away from one of the file cabinet drawers.

Vinnie brought his foot down hard on Joelle's toes.

"*Aaaii!*" the girl cried out in pained surprise.

Terrell's head snapped up sharply,

his eyes focused on Joelle. Then Vinnie yanked open the file drawer with all his might. As the heavy drawer shot out, it smashed into Terrell's shoulder.

Shocked, Terrell grunted in pain and staggered. Vinnie leaped forward quickly and pushed the man to the ground.

Joelle grabbed at the gun and yanked it from his fingers.

Vinnie jumped up from the floor. "You take it!" Joelle cried, shoving the gun in his hand.

Terrell got up, his face twisted with pain. He glared at Vinnie, but he didn't look frightened. "Now what?" he said. "You gonna shoot me?"

"Get in the locker room," Vinnie said.

Terrell moved slowly toward the locker room. "Use your head, Vinnie. You'll be in a lot less trouble if you put down that gun," he said.

"I know," Vinnie said, "but you didn't give me any choice. Okay, Terrell—give me the key."

Terrell gave him a hard look and sighed. But he removed the key from the heavy ring on his belt.

Vinnie opened the locker room door. "Get in," he said.

Terrell stepped inside. "Hope you like *prison,* loser," he growled.

Vinnie said nothing, but hearing the word *prison* gave him a cold, heavy lump in his stomach. He shut the door and locked it.

Vinnie dropped both the gun and the key to the floor. "Run, Joelle!" he cried. "I'm sure he's tripped the silent alarm. The cops'll be here quick."

They raced out of the gym and down the hall toward the front door. The bright lights and tall windows of the lobby made Vinnie feel exposed. Finally, they came to the front door. But as Vinnie reached to open it, someone on the outside started to knock.

"*Police!* Anybody in there?" a woman's voice called out.

Vinnie and Joelle dropped to the floor and crept away as quietly as they could. On the other side of the door, the woman and a man spoke in low voices.

Joelle pointed to the high counter. As quietly as they could, they scuttled past it on their hands and knees. Then they crouched behind the receptionist's desk.

Vinnie looked at Joelle. Her breath was coming fast and hard. Her face had a blank look of disbelief—as if what was happening couldn't be real.

After several long moments, they heard the cops walk away from the door. They forced themselves to wait a few more minutes. Then they got up, and Vinnie cracked open the door.

They took a few cautious steps out to the sidewalk. The patrol car was parked outside, empty. They looked around the corner. On the side of the building, the female police officer was pulling herself through the open window.

"*Run!*" whispered Joelle. They turned

in the opposite direction and took off. They ran block after block, stopping only to catch their breath before running on. Whenever a car approached, they crouched behind a parked car until it went by, and then took off again. Vinnie's chest was burning. The sidewalk in front of him started to blurr.

Vinnie had no idea where they were heading until Joelle panted, "Over there—the park!"

Vinnie's legs ached, and his feet felt like they were on fire. But at last he saw the trees in the park up ahead.

Gasping, they limped to a bench and flopped down. Vinnie turned to Joelle and saw tears flowing down her cheeks.

"Joelle . . . " he said.

The exhausted girl lowered her face to her hands and sobbed as if her heart would break.

# Chapter 8

Vinnie put his arm around Joelle's shoulders. At first he was surprised that she let him. But then he figured she was simply too upset to object.

It was a long time before her sobs finally died away. Vinnie gave her his T-shirt to wipe her face.

"Joelle, I am so sorry," he said.

"Oh, it's not your fault," she said. "I wanted to do it. It's just that I really loved working there."

"I know," he said.

They sat in miserable silence until they started to feel the cold. Then they walked, their sore feet throbbing with every step. Finally, they found an all-night donut shop.

Vinnie led Joelle to a table away from

the windows. He cupped his hands around his coffee to warm them. Then he loosened his shoelaces to ease his throbbing feet. The wall clock said 3:17.

The cook and the cashier were deep in conversation about their boss. Vinnie leaned close to Joelle. In a low voice, he said. "Do you want to go to the police? Shall we see if they'll believe our story?"

"Why would they?" Joelle asked.

"Right," said Vinnie. "Tomorrow's the launch day for SoundUp. Today they'll add the final touches, and then the disks will go in the safe. Ken has to make his move tonight—right? We've gotta try one more time."

"Oh, Vinnie!" Joelle moaned. She shook her head slowly as if it hurt even to do that.

"Come on, Joelle. What have we got to lose?" said Vinnie softly.

She gave him a bleak look.

They sat in the donut shop until the sun came up. At least it was warm inside. Then they slowly walked back to the park. There, they lay on the grass and slept. Vinnie didn't open his eyes until the sun felt hot on his face.

He blinked and sat up with a jerk. Joelle was already awake, watching some kids quarreling over a ball.

"What time is it?" said Vinnie.

"Just about noon," Joelle said, not looking at her watch. She still had the same hopeless look about her.

"Joelle, it's okay if you don't want to go tonight," Vinnie said. "I'll go alone. But I really *want* you to go with me."

"I'm not saying I want to do this," Joelle said. "But what if Ken gets the disk at work somehow? Then he won't be going back to Websound."

"You're right," Vinnie said with a sigh. "We've *got* to follow him. Say, I've got an idea. Does your boyfriend have a car?" Vinnie asked.

Joelle frowned. "I don't want to get him involved," she said.

"But you're in trouble!" said Vinnie.

"Bad idea," Joelle said. "He wouldn't want to hear something like this."

"I'm no expert about people," said Vinnie, "but there's one thing I believe: If you can't go to your boyfriend when you're in trouble, then he's not much of a boyfriend."

Joelle gave him a stubborn look. "You *wish!*" she muttered.

Vinnie shrugged. "I'm gonna go call Olivia," he said. "You gonna be here when I get back?"

"Where else am I going to go?" said Joelle. But Vinnie was glad to see that her look was full of energy now.

Olivia was full of questions that Vinnie didn't want to answer. But she finally agreed to meet him after she picked the kids up from daycare.

Vinnie walked back to Joelle. "My sister's coming with the car. So what do you say, Joelle? Will you come along with me tonight?"

"I will," Joelle said. "But we're going to watch Ken from *outside*. I'm not sneaking in anywhere, okay?"

"Okay, that's a deal," Vinnie said. Just knowing he'd be with Joelle gave him confidence and a lot more hope.

They spent the afternoon quietly. Mostly, they just watched the little kids play on the grass. They were both tired, and there wasn't much to say.

It was just after 6:00 P.M. by the time Olivia pulled up to the curb at the corner of the park.

Vinnie ran over, pulling Joelle by the hand. Olivia took one look at Joelle and shook her head. "Great, Vinnie! Just great!" she said. "You're mixed up in something funny and you won't even tell me about it. And now you're dragging this nice-looking girl into the whole mess. You're gonna end up like Dad—I just know it!"

Vinnie's anger rose, but he didn't dare argue. "Livie," he said, "you gotta trust me! I just can't tell you right now."

Olivia turned to Joelle. "You better ditch this guy. He's bad news."

"*Livie!*" Vinnie protested.

"Just get in and I'll drive us home," Olivia grumbled. "The kids are hungry."

By the time Olivia and the kids were back in their apartment, it was time to head for Websound. Ken usually left the building around 7:00.

They waited across the street from the Websound building as the sky turned from deep blue to black. Sure enough, at 7:10, Ken Castle walked out.

Vinnie watched Ken's long, confident strides. He couldn't help thinking of his own dad—who'd left when he was five and never returned. At first, Ken had seemed like a father to him. Vinnie thought he might be someone to look up to, someone to guide him. Now he watched Ken with something like hate.

Joelle caught his look. "You know what Ken would say, Vinnie," she cautioned. "Don't get mad—get even."

Vinnie managed a sour grin. Joelle was right. He had to keep cool. A few minutes later, Ken drove by in a new green Lexus. Vinnie followed him at a distance, being careful to keep a car or two between them. Ken stopped at an expensive-looking restaurant and sat down alone. Vinnie and Joelle waited impatiently. They were hungry, too, but didn't dare leave the car to buy food.

Finally, they saw Ken get up and leave. Again, they followed his car at a distance. Soon it was clear he was headed back to Websound. They parked a block away.

They waited around for a moment, and then ran all the way to the Websound building. In a minute or two, they were over the fence and skirting the edge of the wide band of concrete around the pool. After crawling over a second fence, they found themselves alongside the low windows of the classrooms. They walked along quietly and peered inside, but the classrooms were dark. In Catherine's office, however, a small light burned.

They edged up to the window. A small safe was turned over on the floor, one end of it neatly sheared open.

"Oh, Vinnie—look!" Joelle gasped. She pointed to a man lying on his back, right next to Catherine's desk!

Vinnie kicked the window with all his strength. It caved in with a crash. Then he kicked around the edges—making a shower of sharp splinters fall onto the bushes!

They ran inside and bent over the fallen man. "Terrell!" Vinnie cried.

The security guard was unconscious and breathing heavily. They could see a nasty bruise on his temple.

Joelle's hand shook as she picked up the phone. "I'll call for help."

Vinnie gave her a longing, sorrowful look. He wanted her safely within his reach every second. But he tore himself away and rushed from the room.

Ken had the disk. He must have just left. Which door did he use? Surely not the door that opened onto the street. Maybe the locker room door. Vinnie ran lightly down the hall and through the gym. Slowly, he pulled open the door to the locker room. He thought he heard a noise—maybe the faint sound of a shoe on the concrete floor. He walked slowly past the tall rows of lockers, one row, two, three, four . . . He jumped when he heard Ken's voice booming out from the back of the room.

"I'm armed, Vinnie!" Ken cried. "Back out of the room *now*, or you're a dead man."

"The cops are coming—for *you*," Vinnie yelled. The cold satisfaction in his voice surprised him.

The door to the patio flew open and Ken charged out. Vinnie raced after him.

As they ran, Vinnie saw Ken shove a

gun into his pocket. Then he leaped up onto the wire fence. When Vinnie grabbed his leg, Ken's free foot came down with a vicious thud on his shoulder. Vinnie gasped from the pain. Shaking loose from Vinnie's grip, Ken reached the top and dropped down into the pool area. Vinnie panted behind him.

Ken raced around the side of the pool. Vinnie followed close behind, the pain in his shoulder forgotten. He grabbed the tail of Ken's shirt. Ken turned and swung. The butt of the gun grazed Vinnie's hair. Then the gun went off with a loud crack, the bullet glancing off the concrete.

Vinnie grabbed Ken's gun arm. With his free hand, Ken pounded his face. Vinnie cringed under the blows, but held on. Then the sight of Ken's face in the harsh lights over the pool made Vinnie white-hot with anger. Bellowing like a madman, he butted his head into Ken's chest as hard as he could.

Ken staggered and fell backward into the pool. There was a hard slapping sound as his body smacked onto the plastic cover. Then the pool cover slowly collapsed and closed over him like a fist. The unconscious man began to sink. The plastic gently rose and fell as Ken thrashed inside it.

Vinnie dove in and tugged at the heavy vinyl. It was heavy as iron. He yanked and pulled as long as he could. Then he came up for air and dove again. He was still doing it when Joelle and the police found him. But by then he was pretty sure that Ken Castle was dead.

The rest of the night was a blur in Vinnie's mind. The police hauled up the pool cover with the help of a winch. When they finally unwrapped the deadly cocoon from around Ken's body, they found the master disk in his pocket. Joelle said something about the disk being water-damaged.

But by then Catherine was there,

telling them she had a copy at home. Catherine also said that Terrell had a mild concussion and was spending the night in the hospital. Around 3 A.M. Olivia came for Vinnie. He got in the car and leaned his head back on the seat. That was all he remembered.

The next day, Saturday, Websound was closed while the police went through the building, collecting evidence. To announce the eagerly anticipated release of SoundUp, Catherine held a press conference at her home.

Ken's funeral was held Tuesday morning. Not many people came—but Vinnie did, even though his shoulder was still bothering him a lot. As he watched the casket being lowered into the ground, he felt that a part of his dream was being buried, too—a part he wanted to forget.

On Wednesday morning, Catherine announced that there was a bidding war for SoundUp. Three record companies were competing to buy the new program. Vinnie noticed that she had already bought a new cover for the pool, but he didn't mention it.

On Friday, SoundUp was bought by EMI. Websound's employees planned a party to celebrate. Vinnie was sent out to get hot dogs. When he returned and walked in the gym, Elizabeth called out, "Here he is!"

Tables were piled high with food. A big banner made from a computer printout read: "THANK YOU, VINNIE!"

As Vinnie walked through the room, everyone turned to him and started clapping loudly. Their faces blurred as he blinked away tears. Joelle walked up to him, a bold look in her eye. "She's going to do it!" he thought to himself. Then all at once her arms were around him and they were kissing. The noise around them swelled to a deafening chorus of whistles and cheers.

COMPREHENSION QUESTIONS

RECALL

1. Who told Vinnie that Web commerce was like the gold rush?

2. What did Joelle say to warn Vinnie about Ken Castle?

3. After breaking in to Websound, where did Vinnie and Joelle spend the night?

NOTING DETAILS

1. What was Ken Castle's password?

2. Besides Websound, what company was about to launch a new music program?

3. Where did the police find the master disk for SoundUp?

DRAWING CONCLUSIONS

1. According to Vinnie, what was Ken Castle's "weak spot"?

2. What conclusion did Vinnie draw about Joelle's boyfriend?

3. What conclusion did Olivia draw about her brother's all-night activities?

IDENTIFYING CHARACTERS

1. Which character in the story claimed to have "cat feet"?

2. Which person at Websound was the only one who didn't wear jeans?

3. Which character had a three-story house and a new sailboat?

VOCABULARY

1. Vinnie was glad to see that Joelle's smile wasn't *predatory*. What does *predatory* mean?

2. Meeting his co-workers, Vinnie couldn't figure out which one could be the *mole*. When used as slang, what does the word *mole* mean?

3. Catherine warned the snooper that he could be charged with a *felony*. What's a *felony*?